The BOY Who LOOKED Like LiNCOLN

For Ken, Ted, Max, Tom, Bob, Sam & Al.—M.R.

For Brian; a Lincoln kinda guy—honestly.—D.C.

PUFFIN BOOKS
Published by the Penguin Group
Penguin Young Readers Group, 345 Hudson Street, New York, New York 10014, U.S.A.
Penguin Group (Canada), 90 Eglinton Avenue East, Suite 700, Toronto, Ontario, Canada M4P 2Y3
(a division of Pearson Penguin Canada Inc.)
Penguin Books Ltd, 80 Strand, London WC2R 0RL, England
Penguin Ireland, 25 St Stephen's Green, Dublin 2, Ireland (a division of Penguin Books Ltd)
Penguin Group (Australia), 250 Camberwell Road, Camberwell, Victoria 3124, Australia
(a division of Pearson Australia Group Pty Ltd)
Penguin Books India Pvt Ltd, 11 Community Centre, Panchsheel Park, New Delhi - 110 017, India
Penguin Group (NZ), Cnr Airborne and Rosedale Roads, Albany, Auckland 1310, New Zealand
(a division of Pearson New Zealand Ltd)
Penguin Books (South Africa) (Pty) Ltd, 24 Sturdee Avenue, Rosebank, Johannesburg 2196, South Africa

Registered Offices: Penguin Books Ltd, 80 Strand, London WC2R 0RL, England

First published by Price Stern Sloan, a division of Penguin Young Readers Group, 2003
Published by Puffin Books, a division of Penguin Young Readers Group, 2006

1 3 5 7 9 10 8 6 4 2

Text copyright © Mike Reiss, 2003
Illustrations copyright © David Catrow, 2003
All rights reserved

THE LIBRARY OF CONGRESS HAS CATALOGED THE PRICE STERN SLOAN EDITION AS FOLLOWS:
Reiss, Mike.
The boy who looked like Lincoln / by Mike Reiss ; illustrated by David Catrow.
p. cm.
Summary: Eight-year-old Benjy, who resembles Abraham Lincoln, is tired of being teased and always
being Lincoln in the school play, but a special camp helps him to appreciate his appearance.
[1. Self-esteem—Fiction. 2. Identity—Fiction. 3. Schools—Fiction.
4. Camps—Fiction.]
I. Catrow, David, ill. II. Title.
PZ7.R2784 Bo 2003 [E]—dc21 2003004712
ISBN 0-8431-0271-3 (hc)

Puffin Books ISBN 0-14-240416-0

Manufactured in China
Designed by Debbie Guy-Christiansen and Giovanni Cipolla

The BOY Who LOOKED Like LINCOLN

By Mike Reiss
Illustrated by David Catrow

PUFFIN BOOKS

My name is Benjy. I'm eight years old. I look a lot like Abe Lincoln.

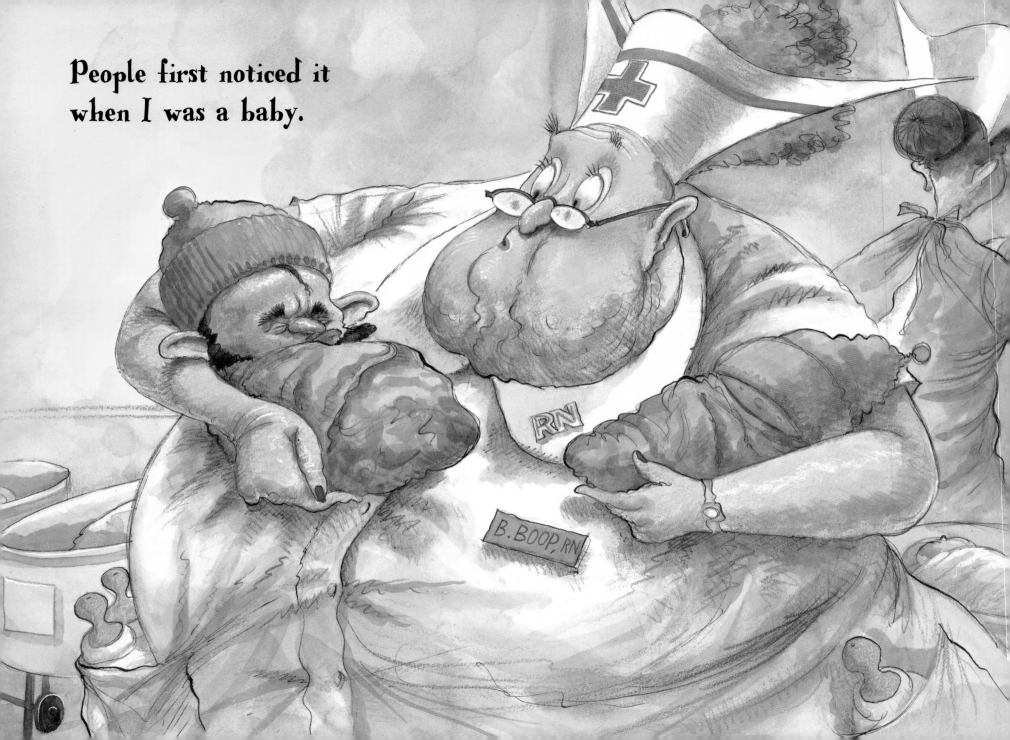

People first noticed it
when I was a baby.

I guess I get it
from my parents.

Every birthday
I get the same gifts.

I even wear the dumb hat. Anything else looks silly on me.

In every school play, I have to be Lincoln.
Even if he's not in the show.

But the worst part is the teasing.

So when school ended, I planned to spend the summer sitting in my room—in the dark.

But my parents had a surprise for me . . .

They took me to a camp.
A special camp . . .

. . . A camp for kids who looked like things.

There was a kid who looked like the Mona Lisa. And a kid who looked like a frog. And one who looked like a toaster.

There was even a kid who looked like the back of a horse. I felt really bad for him. But after a while, you didn't even notice.

We had fun
every day.

And at night, I'd stay up late and read about Lincoln. He was a pretty cool guy.

I made a lot of friends that summer.

And so did the kid who looked like a horse's butt.

On the last day of camp my parents picked me up. "You look happy," said my Dad. "You need a haircut," said my Mom.

When I went back to school, I felt a lot better.

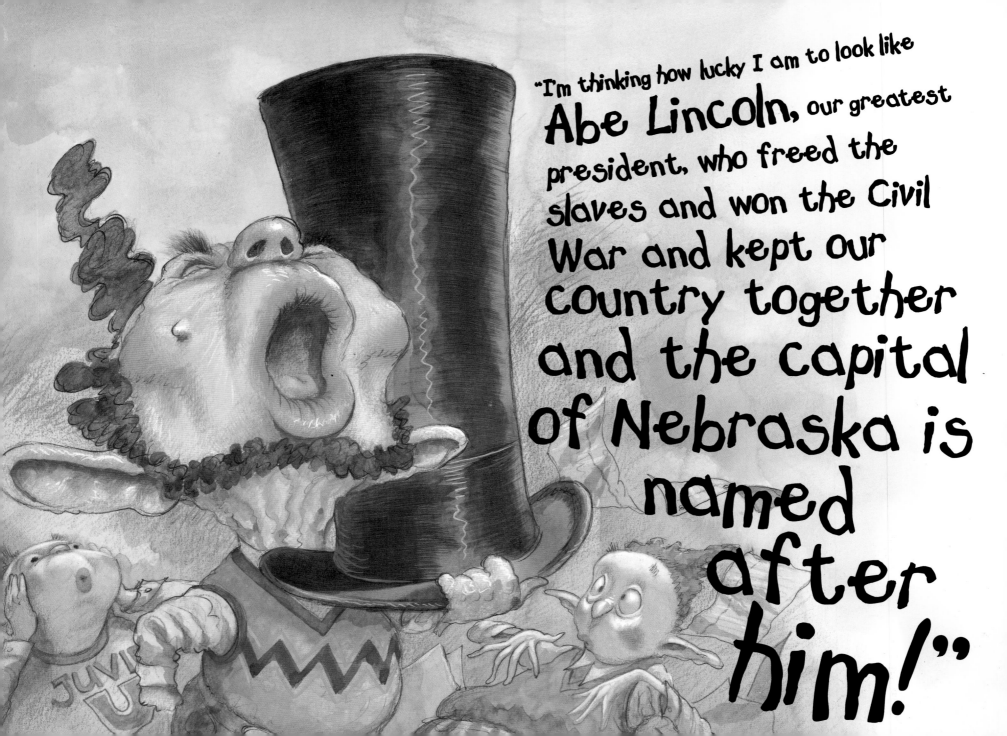

"I'm thinking how lucky I am to look like Abe Lincoln, our greatest president, who freed the slaves and won the Civil War and kept our country together and the capital of Nebraska is named after him!"

I guess your face is one thing
that makes you special.
I hope you like yours.
I know I like mine. . .

And I think it may have helped get me elected class president this year.

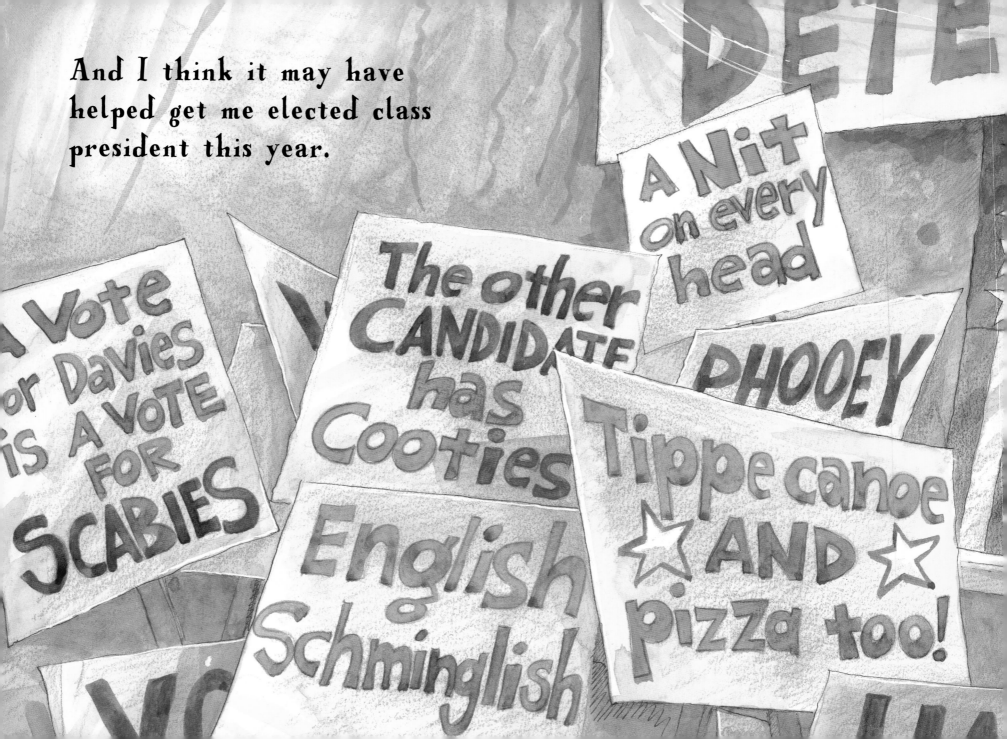

MORE POP
FEWER POP QUIZZES
THE Pink AYES HAVE IT
Elect Leonard Zeeler
teacher's PET

Now I just have to figure out how to help my baby brother, Dickie.